Community D!@k

Author Tray Real

Published by Author Tray Real, 2023.

COMMUNITY D!@K

First edition. September 27, 2023.

ISBN: 979-8223334446

Written by Author Tray Real.

I dedicate this book to my friends who've allowed me to have fun with this one. I put y'all all up in here. Thanks for the support.

My pen bleeds ink from my heart.

I'm not wasting another summer on a low-life cheating ass nigga or trying to differentiate the difference between a man and a nigga! It's scary not knowing off of the rip because we meet the imposter first. There's not always a tale tale sign up front, or a hint as to what one's intension are for your life. But Ah bitch is tired, and I'm done wasting time on Gawd! The lies, false promises, the side bitches, and the disrespect is too much to give for the return. Meech has got to get the fuck on A.S.A.P! The more I tried believing in his raggedy ass, the more he lied and cheated. Me staying and just fussing about the shit, without some type of recourse, made him worse and wasn't the answer. He went from being verbally abusive to threatening to physically harm me. All lines have been drawn and crossed! I'm about to break his entire life down in slow motion. The next time he decides to play with another woman in this community, he will think twice.

Just looking at Meech, you'd be like DAAMMN, he's fine as hell! And that's because he is. Meech has a body of a God, and his style of dress is fire. You'd think when looking at him that he was well put together.

When I first met him, I met his intellectual imposter that had a dash of hood. I had no idea, nor would I have ever thought that he was arrogant as hell, and the type of nigga that refuses to accept that his player card had been trumped and revoked!

He is partial blame for why nigga's like him, create bitches like me, and our heartless demeanor. They don't appreciate us, women, for who we are, therefore, they continue doing us dirty, and can't stand up in the dirt them damn selves. Don't get me wrong, there are definitely some bitches who were born heartless. It's in their D.N.A. I'm not talkin' 'bout them, that's an entirely different book. I'm talkin' bout us bitches who don't mind taking the teacher back to school because of what she was taught in life while fucking with a bitch ass nigga. After being taken for granted so many times, we have to learn to protect ourselves better. Men do what we allow and accept. Some of us build walls of protection up, keeping out anyone and anything not bringing peace to the home front. All of us need to be doing it!

It's either that, or I'm just letting my motherfuckin' dogs loose because I'm drained! My bruhs are my dogs, and anyone of them will have Meech ass up stank somewhere for fuckin over me! I just kept it on the low to keep my bruhs from doing time behind their only sister's community dick ass nigga!

I partially blame myself and hold myself responsible for allowing him to treat me like this. I have to be accountable for putting up with his shit, renaming it, and calling it love. In reality, it was loveless bullshit and control that kept me playing the game. It's time to let the community have his ass, Meech must go! If you don't know me, or ah bitch like me, then you will! My name is Candy, but it doesn't mean that Ima sucka!

Some of these hoes are just as nasty as these nigga's! They'll trick with any and everyone's man just to get a bag or a wet ass. Ignorance has allowed these bitches to pull up with audacity, and stalk you like you are the problem and not the nigga in question. There is no defending that dumb shit! I've never understood why females get mad at the female and not the nigga they have the relationship with! Riddle me that, cause that has never made any sense to me. Honestly, it's weird ass fuck! I've gotten into more fights than the law allows behind the hyping of weird shit. My situation is the perfect case in point. The bitches always come looking for me, and not Meech. He's the one that sold them pipe dreams, and I had to be the dream interpreter. Hoes were popping up at the house or pulling up at the park just to be stomped out by a real one, cause BABY, I ain't taking no "L" behind no community dick ass nigga! You can put that on Mary and her ugly ass lil lamb!

The last few times Meech has cheated were crazy. I didn't know he was cheating but I definitely suspected it. His routine began changing, and his attitude and demeanor exposed what the streets were saying. Meech always tended to cheat with low-budget bitches that he could control out of one of the projects. These last few incidents took the cake and the icing. I hadn't slept with Meech in weeks at this point, something told me to stop making myself so convenient for him. Especially since he was too busy to take me out or spend real time with me. My head told me that it was over, and the streets told me why I was right.

Meech messed around with the NuNu twins. Neither sister knew that he messed with the other per the streets. Well, shit hit the fan when one sister had crabs and VD, and the other had Trichomonas and crabs landing all three at the clinic on the same damn day. The sisters purposely made appointments on the same day in order to ride together. They complained about how nasty the nigga's they had been fucking were, and how much pain they were in. Those crabs were biting the shit out of em! They claimed they were done messing around with these hood niggas for a little coin, neither purposely not mentioning their nigga's name. They both feared saying who he was because they knew Meech's street reputation, and knew if word got out, he would try killing them.

The twins were seen first. Each given their diagnosis and medication. Once they exited out of the exam rooms, both genuinely upset, they waited for the other in the sitting area. As they approached the exit, Meech was entering. When I say "if beat a nigga on sight had a name" it would be NuNu twins. When I say those big bitches got with that nigga, they got with him like all three were fighting over a happy meal. They tried killing him before he even knew what was going on.

He had no time to prepare, duck, or run out. The security for the doctors building all had to try and break it up. They called for backup who eventually peeled Meech out of the corner. He claimed that he didn't hit them back, per his boys, because he didn't want to go to jail for domestic violence, but the twins were charged. None of them are allowed back at the doctor's office. Meech was seen and treated for his diseases and wounds at a nearby hospital. Once he was seen and released, he shot up both of their homes. The twins were evicted due to their felonious charges. They were sentenced to county jail for thirteen months. While Meech still hadn't learned his lesson.

"STOP CALLING MY MOTHERFUCKIN PHONE bitch! I really don't give a fuck! if you want the dog ass nigga then keep him over there! No need in calling and playing games on my phone!" I hate when ah bitch, a simple bitch at that, has too much free time! "Lose my number lil ugly before I blow down and stump yo ass the fuck out!" I yelled furiously before hanging up my end.

I need to get my ass in the shower and throw on some clothes. I'm about to pack Meeches shit up and dump it right in the damn projects! Let whichever hoe he's with this week sort it all out. Evidently, he is somewhere in the vicinity or touched down and left. I draw the line today, this was it! I have too much going on to allow myself to be pulled down by a nigga that has no up's in his blood. The community can have his limp tired dick because I feel nothing!

The only way the bitch could have gotten my number is if he touched down at her crib and laid his phone down. She had to have taken my number out of his phone because my number is new and private. That's exactly why the bum ass nigga hasn't brought his ass around here. He is a certified liar! Let him tell the story, I'm tripping. He's been out making money throughout the nights. He had better not bring his ass over here talking that baby this, baby that bullshit either, or these hot grits are about to get him all the way together. Let this be the motherfuckin' day!

Knock, knock, knock! "Who is it?" I asked although I already knew the answer. "Baby, it's me!" Meech began yelling. "Let me in!" I paused for a minute just for the effects because I knew the bum was coming. He knew and I knew that he wasn't getting up in here this time. "Oh, hell nawl, you can stop calling me baby, BUM! It's a wrap for you over here playboy! Get off my property right motherfuckin' now! You can't play or stay here not one more day! Take your ass back to the projects where you belong! I've told you over and over that I don't fuck with community dick! You got the game twisted, my nigga! Get the hell away from my door disturbing the peace!" I yelled.

"Bitch!" Meech screamed through gritted teeth. " Stop talking so gotdamn much and open this door before I kick it off the hinges!" When he said that, I went straight into the kitchen and turned on my aisles. One had grits, and the other had grease on it. I wanted his ass to try anything, and it was going down. He continued screaming and banging on my door as though I hadn't said a motherfuckin' word! I guess he didn't hear shit I said. While he continued acting out, I sent a text to Lil Gucci, one of my ruthless ass brothers, telling him that Meech was trying to break in and that he's threatening me! I knew my brother was in the vicinity gambling. He was always close by. I then stood in my kitchen stirring the grits in anticipation, before I yelled," Kick then nigga because I'm..." BOOM!

"Where the fuck you at? You had so much to say while I was outside!" Meech began yelling. " I told you bitch; you can't keep me out of my own motherfuckin' house! I run this shit and I run you!" No, he didn't just say RUN, BITCH, or his HOUSE in the same sentence! I bought this house myself without his or any of my brother's help. He's about to be a witness to why when a female has no more emotional ties, and she is tired, as well as fed up, her done game will cause the hardest of niggas to become bitches! "I'm grown nigga, so I say what I want, you gets no respect from me! I'm in here punk, I'm not hard to find in my own house. Come make me know what you just said, 'cause the only thing I know is, you didn't just kick my door in!" I began responding to his antics.

"That was lightweight stupid! You know like I know that this isn't your home, it's mine! I haven't seen you in weeks, and now you want to show up on this bullshit, I don't think so! I had a feeling you were coming; I just didn't know when. It's okay though. We're about to see who the real bitch is." I continued saying in a monotone. "Where are you?" Meech called out as he did his walk from my living room to my bedrooms, and finally the kitchen. "You can't hide ahhhh! ahhhhh! My eyes ahhhhh! Candy what the fuck!" he screamed. "Yeah nigga, that's them grits! Keep talking and this hot grease is next!" I said as I picked up the pot with the hot grease in it, ready when you are!" I said like a boss protecting her investment. "Candy, I'm beating your ass!"

"Sup Candy?" my brother Lil Gucci asked as he walked right through the living room and past me, into the kitchen, and over to Meeches screaming ass. My brother began cracking his jaw in anger as he walked over slowly to where Meech sat talking shit in a mumble and holding his face. "Shut the fuck up nigga! What did I tell you about how you handle my sister, pussy boy?! Didn't we talk about this shit nigga?" My brother asked. "Gucci man listen," Meech began, "I wasn't going to touch her. I was just going to scare her a little man, that's it!" he continued explaining like a bitch. "Well," Lil Gucci said through gritted teeth. "My sister doesn't like being scared. After you take this ass-kicking for being hardheaded, you are going to fix her door, and give her back her key, deal!" CRACK!!

It has been over a year since Lil Gucci beat the brakes out of Meech. There hasn't been any sightings of him since. The only thing I do know is, he couldn't fix my door that day. My brothers called over a couple of their goons to do it and change the locks. They also installed security cameras in order for my brothers to keep tabs on me. After Lil Gucci beat the brakes out of Meech, their goons also carried Meech away from here. I heard on the streets that they dumped Meech on the porch of the chic who called playing on my phone. Lil Gucci never spoke about it, but the streets said that he had a note laid on Meech that read: "You can have this nigga, he can't fight or fuck!" I believe Lil Gucci did that shit or orchestrated it; he is certified crazy. The hoe was not happy about none of our shenanigans. She attempted to try playing the game back on her beat-up nigga's behalf. She in turn showed up at my house and put a note on my door saying that she was going to kill me. I reported her simple ass to the housing authorities which caused her to get evicted. The hoe went by Bullet. Once Bullet was evicted, she disappeared off into LaLa land, but I knew this wasn't over. I knew one day that she would resurface on the same dumb shit.

My brothers were overprotective of me. I am the only girl, and baby girl under five brothers. My government name is Candace, but everyone calls me Candy. My five brothers are Big V, Big Ro, Lil Gucci, PI, and Bleep. We were raised by our aunts Big Ren and Nelli after our mother passed away. I was in the seventh grade and took it the hardest. Although I was daddy's girl, I haven't seen our dad since I was nine years old. Our father is on Rikers Island fighting his last appeal. My brothers hired him a high-profile attorney out of Canada. I never understood why our dad would not allow us to come and see him. I would ask and sometimes plead. The answer was always no. Our dad wanted to do his time alone. He said that in order to keep his head on right, he had to forget that he had family outside of those walls. Emotionally he had to shut himself down. The only thing that he would allow from time to time is pictures or a letter here and there. Long story short, he was in the mob and the mob got busted. He has been serving time for bodies that were pinned on him with no evidence.

My Aunts did the best they could with raising us. Although I was the only girl out of my siblings, my aunts had girls. I had girl cousins who grew up as a motherfuckin' gang themselves. I was schooled and hung out with them. Shell, Ya, Tip, and Lisha are my cousin sisters. We grew up making shit happen point blank and period!

Three out of my five brothers own the largest strip club in LA. They spend a lot of time taking care of everyday issues and make a lot of money. The other two keep the streets on point and make sure that the ladies in the fam are always good. Together we are our own wrecking crew.

My brothers schooled me on "the game." Yet, I kept getting caught up with the same "for everybody" ass nigga's because I was hard-headed and kept attracting the same type of nigga. I didn't realize that I was allowing these nigga's to lower my self-esteem and my standards. I had too much to offer to settle for anything. Hell, I blamed it on the weed. I smoked too much weed, and weed made me want what I wanted. Now I'm working on my wants not superseding my needs. I'm working on improving that area of my life, so now I go shopping when I get an urge.

I guess I had better get up and get moving. The mall is calling my name. Meech and his mess still got my nerves on ten after a year had gone by. I haven't let my guard down or dated. I am taking time out to work on myself. It's not over, I know him! Meech is vengeful and patient, he's coming! I'm staying strapped and ready to blow that nigga back to his ancestors! My finger stays on the trigger. After I hit this blunt, I'll call my girls to see what's popping off on the Hill Top. They may want to roll with me to the mall.

"Hey, Sis, who got that bag?" I asked Reesie. Reesie started laughing before she responded back, "It's some hoes in this house! It's some hoes in this house!" We both burst out laughing because we knew a few scrubs were on the block holding their bags and slanging ding-a-ling on a promise. "That's what I thought!" I stated. "What y'all doing?" I asked Reesie. "Dream over on the stoop hugged up with Regg, and Thick was just at it with them Valley girls. Bitch, I'm waiting for Hitman to roll his ass up over here to drop off some more Cookie," she began saying. "What are you getting into Chicca?" Reesie asked. "I am about to head to the mall. My brothers got something going on tonight at the spot, and I need to find a little scandal to put on. Thinking back bitch, I should have hit up Beat The Odd's two, but it's too late for that afterthought shit," I said regretting that I hadn't thought of it sooner. "Come and get us hoe! We rolling with you," Reesie suggested. I knew they would want to roll, that's what we do. "Alright, give me thirty minutes and I'll be pulling up hoe. Let Thick know, we not fuckin up bitches today, ain't nobody on that bullshit! Let them wacky tramps from the 'V' stay wacky in the "V." Reesie as usual was cracking up. "Okay girl, but you know Sis be busting heads, and don't ask questions about shit!" she said. "Right,

I agreed! But not at the mall, we need to get ready for tonight. Let me throw something on really quick," I said laughingly.

Damn, It's a beautiful day outside. As I rolled through the neighborhood, I noticed that everybody who was anybody was hanging out. Lil Ronnie's spot had all the bikes out. We might have to roll back through when we leave the mall. It felt good as hell riding around with the top down. I had my old-school joints blaring from my speakers as I took in and enjoyed the scenario. As I got closer to the Hilltop, I was hoping them hoes were ready when I pulled up. Sometimes they be on that "give me a second bullshit." I don't have seconds to give, I do got hours for my bitches if that's what they need, I thought as I laughed a little. All my sister girls are solid except one. Her energy doesn't sit right with me.

As I pulled up on the hill, I saw a big crowd. I hope my girls aren't in whatever that shit is. Oh, I see Thick. "Hey, Thick!" I screamed. Thick walked over like only she could walk. My sister cracks me up." What's up, Sis?' Thick asked. "Shit," I responded. 'Where is everybody?" I asked. "Reesie and Dream over there watching a fight." I looked in the direction that she pointed. "It is too damn hot to be out here fighting! Who out here on that she and why?" I asked. "Shit bitch, I don't know facts, only what I heard. They said Niecy's dude was messing around with some sneaky link from that Harvard area. That must be the girl she's fighting because she asked the girl about it, and the next thing you know; they were pulling wigs and gauging eyes," Thick explained. "What the fuck!" I said in shock!

"That's not like Niecy. I am stunned by that mess," I said. "Right," Thick began responding. "That's not even the killer though. That nigga Chill that use to be with Meech resurfaced. He is who Niecy fucking with and who they are beefing over. "Chill" they are fighting over pull up on the scene with his boy Dub riding co-pilot and two of those drunk uglies from Harvard in the back seat. He pulled up where the fight was and started laughing at Niecy and the girl and then said they looked stupid as hell! He spun his tires out down the parking lot with the uglies Niecy thinks are her friends. They were in the backseat laughing with full cups appearing high as hell. It couldn't be me is all that I could say. I then told Thick to tell the girls we have shit to do and let's bounce. It's too nice of a day to waste on bull crap. Alright, Thick said. Give me a sec.

We rolled and caught up on the street gossip. While my girls shared the street scoop, I kind of drifted off in thought. It was weird because just recently, I started getting an eerie unexplainable feeling. Which is what snapped me out of thought. I shook it off as we continued to the mall to find something to wear for tonight.

The mall's parking lot was packed. We had to walk a long way to the door. We laughed and talked catching up still. Dream interrupted everything by saying," Candy girl, I meant to call you last night. I saw your Boo Meech back on scene girl. He was sporting a BMW M5 Hurricane G-Power RS. Girl, he got out at that new spot 4300. It was a few cars of us out parking lot pimping and BAM...he drove up. Everybody's mouths dropped. Chile, he is bald now. He looked as though he ate, slept, and drank weights. His body is buff as fuck. He was dressed to the hills from head to motherfucking toe in designer. Girl, you know your hot fake-ass cousins needed some attention and were the first on scene trying to get at him. When he turned around to see who was calling his name, he smiled with pearly whites and had the nerve to remove his glasses and those hazel eyes had them bitches laying on the AstroTurf. I looked at Dream and shook my head. She had too much detail not to be interested and entertained herself. Out of all my girls, that's the one that would do some ignorant shit and end up getting these hands. He spoke to me, and I spoke back. I don't have shit to do with what happened with y'all. This instantly pissed me off. I turned to her and said, "No bitch you don't! You might want to tread lightly though. Being my girl or being considered a friend to me is not a part-time gig. You cross me and fuck behind me and it's a wrap! I'm just letting you know off the rip and not saying that those are your intentions. Ya dig, so no need to get hyped up about any man I axed out. He was a cute, sexy abuser when I fucked with him over a year ago. If his insides are still the same, he still isn't shit. Now I'm done talking about it!

We continued to walk up to the mall entrance, it was nothing but silence until Thick had an outburst. We all looked at her trying to figure out what in the world she was doing or saying. She burst out laughing asking us what? I shook my head because I knew what she was thinking. We decided to split up and meet back in the middle of the mall in two hours. Me and Thick basically ended up staying together as did Dream and Reesie. I found a bad body suit at the BDO2 store that was fierce. Thank God it wasn't too late, and they were not closed. It was only two made and they said a lady from New York had come and bought the other one earlier that day. I bought some snakeskin six-inch green bottoms that matched perfectly. Thick found this two-piece skirt set that was sheer and fire. She found her shoes and we left after spending a grip in search of our accessories. I called Hair by him to see if I could squeeze two of us in with him and we called Peniel's to see if the owner had two spots open. It was about to go down! Our nails and feet were just done a day or so ago, so that was cool.

Candy! I turned around looking for the familiar voice, but I saw no one. Me and Thick kept walking. Oh, so you can't speak now! Thick and I both heard this comment stopped dead in our tracks and turned around. Meech was looking straight in my face. He had Chill and a couple of thugs from Chicago with him slinging off his Vienna. "Sup Meech," I responded. He went on with some jibber jabber about wanting to apologize for doing me wrong. He even took it an extra mile further by saying if my brothers hadn't...Brothers? I questioned in front of his boys. My brothers didn't do shit! My brother only stopped you from continuously trying to fight me and tearing my house up! You remember the door you kicked off the hinges, right? A couple of his boys looked dumbfounded while Chill laughed. They looked from me to him for answers. Look baby Meech began," It's all water under the bridge. Can you forgive me?" I said, yeah whatever Meech and then turned and walked off. There's that uneasy feeling again. I felt this before but couldn't put my finger on it. I looked around and saw nothing out of character or suspicious. Thick was still talking to one of Meech's boys, so I called for Thick to come on. We need to meet up with the other girls. She was being entertained by a couple of the fellas and exchanged numbers with one giving him Dream's number instead of her own. We headed back to meet up with Reesie and Dream. Reese looked relieved. We checked out both of their outfits and as usual, Dream had the hoe game faded. Reesie was more casual, but she had great taste. We stopped on our way out the door in Macy's to get our accessories and then we bounced.

On our ride back, we discussed our split up of two and two to get our hair and make-up done. Our approximate time of our meet up and who was all driving later etc. We decided that everyone would drive to my spot, and we'd take one car. You can probably guess whose car.

Reesie suggested that everyone meet up at my spot early so that we could smoke and get our drink on." Cool", we agreed. We all went and got our hair and make-up done. It was starting to get late. I rushed everyone home so that we could all get our showers and start to get ready. Time was ticking and the excitement of the night's events was starting to get me geeked. I smoked a blunt and turned on my old school all-time favorite EZM CD and danced until I started to sweat a little. Let me sit my ass down somewhere before I must take another shower, I told myself. My doorbell began buzzing. I turned the music down a little just to say, "Here I come." It was Reesie smiling and laughing as usual. Hey, Reesie Cup, you are looking stunning I stated. She responded with, "Thank you Candy girl." We both started giggling as I invited her in for a drink. "Would you like a drink and some refreshments Ms. Reesie?" "Sure," she replied. I brought out the Patron and some Vanilla Crown. I waited for Thick to bring out the Peach Cîroc and Dream drinks that stinky 1800 Silver. One by one they blew down. I provided chicken wings I had ordered earlier that evening. I had some finger sandwiches, pretzels, and some chips. We smoked and had a few shots, now it was time to roll.

We pulled up on the street of the club and you couldn't even get on the street. I immediately called my brother Big Vee. No answer. I called PI, no answer. I called Big Ro. Hello, Ro, I'm stuck all the way down Main St. I'm with the girls. I need someone to get me to the parking garage. Ro responded with," Say less" and hung up his line. I promise you it wasn't ten minutes later that Bleep and Lil Gucci came and personally made sure that all cars were pulled over so that my car had full access to the street. That was a power move If I had ever seen one. They gave no fucks if cars sat on the backs of the one in front of theirs if I was able to get by. Once we pulled up to the garage entrance, we were escorted out of my car and into the club. My brothers took my car leaving their bikes with their workers. The girls were quiet and in amazement. My brothers loved me to death as I loved them. We were tight. I stayed out of their way and they respected my space.

The strip club's name was "The Drizzle." When we walked in I almost fainted. I hadn't been inside since the renovation in which I helped install the security cameras. It was the nicest club I had ever entered in my life. The dancers were on fire! This wasn't "Pink," but the dancers were on fire like it was. Money was everywhere and I mean everywhere. Celebrities were in the heavily guarded, bullet-proof V.I.P. area. There was a big eating area that served everything from crab to lobster, gumbo to collard greens on the far side. Closer to where we were was a nice dance floor that was roped off so that the dancing wouldn't interfere with the patrons who just wanted to chill. Tonight, had special guests who were about to grace the stage. We found seats right in time. We ordered our drinks and some hors d'oeuvres. Hot-ass Dream also put in an order for a lap dance. Thick looked over at me and rolled her eyes. I started laughing a little when Thick mumbled, "hot ass always got to be the extra one." We all danced in our seats for a few more minutes until a waitress came over with a bottle of Moet and said, "compliments of the gentlemen behind you." We all turned in unison to see who the gentlemen were. I was pissed and unmoved. I said, "Please return to sender Ms., and tell him and his crew thanks but no thanks." Fuck that Dream shouted! I'm keeping it. You don't have to touch this poison. I will give this bottle all the hands it needs. Thick stood up and said, "I'm sick of your raggedy thirsty ass. You are a thirst trap!" "Go ahead and drink it, when you fall over poisoned don't look for us to pick you up. I can't stand your irritating ass sometimes bitch." You could hear Meech and his boys laughing at the exchange. I could feel him breathing down my neck. Hey Dream, Meeches boy Jax called out. Come back here with us baby. We will make sure you're good. Reesie looked on in amazement as that simple bitch Dream went and sat with all those guys. She thought that she was a bad bitch, not realizing that she was just some tuna amongst sharks!

CHAPTER FIVE

I couldn't even focus on the show when Genuine, Tank, Tyrese, and Nelly hit the stage. Everybody and their mama started stripping when Nelly started singing, "It's getting hot in here," Bras, drawls, shirts, shorts, money everything was flying. The Hoe Dream purposely threw her bra our way. It landed on Reesie's shoulder. The guys thought it was funny. Reesie just knocked it off and looked back. She looked back in time enough to see Dream lip-locked with Meech. At first, Reesie didn't say anything. She just shook her knee. I knew then that something wasn't right. I turned slightly enough to catch the end of the lip lock out of my peripheral. Just behind the principal of it, I whispered what we witnessed to Thick. She sat motionless for a few minutes. When Genuine followed up with riding his pony, I noticed that Dream had gotten up and started circulating the room. People were going wild. It was wall-to-wall people everywhere. Security was on high alert and my brothers had everything covered. I noticed that my brother PI and Lil Gucci were sitting off to the side of us in the cut. I didn't notice them before. I also began looking around and to my surprise they had us surrounded with their best undercover team. Over our heads, the cameras were zooming in and out. No one really paid them any attention because if you didn't know that they were there you couldn't see them. But I helped install them, so I knew where most were.

There was that feeling again. Damn, now it's starting to irritate the crap out of me! Why do I keep feeling like someone is watching me? I had my gun in my purse cocked and loaded just in case. My stupid ass question is, "Who the fuck am I going to shoot?". There are no familiar faces anywhere.

We all got up and danced during remission. A guy from the Bronx I've seen in there and around town before came and asked me for a dance. We danced and laughed, making small talk, and just enjoying one another's company. Thick and Reesie also snagged a couple of nice-looking guys in town on business. All were mannerable and very respectful. They asked if they could join us to finish out the night. We laughed and danced until we couldn't do either anymore. We exchanged numbers and promised to all hang out the next day. They promised to call after they were finished with their business.

Dreams nightmare

Reesie leaned in and asked me if had I seen Dream. Although we are mad at her, we still wouldn't want to see harm brought to her. I spoke. "No, I haven't seen her in a while." I leaned over and asked the same question to Thick. Thick said, "We need to go see if she is in the bathroom or something. It's been almost an hour since she walked off." Meech neem left too. Reesie jumped up and said that she'd be right back. We both told her she had five minutes and then we would be coming to look for her.

I watched as Lil Gucci jumped up to catch up with Reesie. I think he is sweet on her. A couple of his boys were with him. ``Where are you going Lil momma? Gucci asked Reesie after catching up with her." Hey Gucci," Reesie replied. "I'm looking for Dream. We haven't seen her in over an hour." "Is that right," Gucci responded back. Gucci whispered something to the guys that were with him, and they split up searching high and low.

Reesie

There was a long line going to the lady's bathroom that shouldn't have even existed. This was my first hint that something wasn't right. This place had four humongous ladies' restrooms with several stalls that stayed sanitized. I barged to the front of the line and heard muffled laughs and screams. I pushed on the door, but it wouldn't budge. It felt like someone, or something was blocking it. I got on the phone and called Candy and Thick and told Candy to hit her brothers up. I politely took out my 357 and shot through the door. Whoever was blocking the door was about to get a new ass hole. I heard the scream and felt the release. I kicked the door open just as Meech had Dream bent over the sink finishing up fucking her in her ass. The dude I shot had fallen to the floor in agony and pain. No one paid him any attention because their attention was on Meech and the rape that was taken place by his perverted ass. You can tell she was out of it as three other guys stood around with their Vienna's out jacking them off ready for next. I shot another warning shot and some buster with no aim shot back at me. Gucci and his security team came, and bum rushed the bathroom guns blazing. Instead of killing the motherfuckas they pistol whipped the shit out of all of them. Meech got it the worst. Thick and Candy helped me get Dream up and out of harm's way. She was damaged. They mutilated that girl and laughed about it. I heard them laughing when I was trying to gain access. We need to get her some medical treatment. PI and Bleep walked up and took her from us. Both reassuring us that they had her. They were going to make sure that she received top-notch medical treatment. Big Ro and Big Vee escorted us to Candy's house. They had security drive her car to her house. The security team entered Candy's home and performed a perimeter and security check on the outside. They instructed all of us to stay there for the night. We did as we were told. None of us could sleep. We sat up in her living room replaying the night's events until mid-morning. Eventually, we all passed out from being overly exhausted, worried, and just mentally screwed.

The sun came up at 7:05 a.m. It appears we had just gone to sleep, and we truly did. We heard keys in the door. So, we all grabbed our straps and took cover. Thick yelled out, 'It's too early for this shit, DAMN!' until she saw the smorgasbord that my brothers were bringing in. We all started laughing as we all grabbed for a blunt or mild ready to light up." How y'all ladies feel?" asked Lil Gucci." We are good brothers," I replied. "Good morning, Reesie Cup," he turned to pay her extra attention. We all laughed as she blushed and smiled like a Chia pet. He took a seat next to her and whispered something to her that had her hitting him on the arm jokingly. PI bow-guarded his big self over to Thick, picked her up, and sat her on his lap. We were crying and laughing! He then had one of the guys that rode with them fix them a plate. We laughed and laughed until we couldn't laugh anymore. I got up and turned on some old-school R&B. We listened to some soothing music as we talked about what had happened and how Dream was.

Lil Gucci began with, "Big Ren and Nelli have stepped in. They have Dream, so she's good. We sent in Shell, Tip, Ya, and Lisha to unravel the biggest mystery. "What's that?" I asked my brother. Meech wants REVENGE. "You remember the chic's apartment we dumped him at?," Lil Gucci asked. Well, she got reported and put out on the streets. She said that you did it, Candy. She had nowhere to go. She lost custody of her kids, so she put that pussy to work and hit a jackpot. She became a millionaire's slut. Her Millionaire pimp spent millions on her and completely changed her looks. You would never know who she is because she was schooled on charm and how she presents herself. Her skin is even light enough to pass for white. The one thing about a hood bitch though is, she will always be hood. I don't give a fuck what she replaces on her body her hood mindset will remain intact. Anyway, she brought Meech in as her brother. He was the community penis and slept with all the rich white folk but couldn't hit a jackpot like her. She paid top dollar to get Meeches to look on point. She also spent thousands on his cars, clothes, and anything of value that he thought of. She did all this under one condition.' What was that condition?" I asked out of curiosity. The condition was that he was never to come back to you Candy.' Do y'all know what got me stumped? "Lil Gucci asked. "No," Thick responded. Tell us. What got me stumped is the fact that she knows he has three of those women pregnant with his seed but has this obsession with wanting to hurt Candy. Don't laugh, but I think Meech is on a mission called "Candy Crush."

We all sat around shaking our heads and mumbling at the bitch's obsession. Thick then asked no one in particular. "Uhm, does anyone happen to know the bitches name? We've all referred to her as bitch and hoe and not one time has anyone said what her name was or who she is related to if anyone in the projects. Somebody knows more than what's being said." Thick then looked in my direction as if I were supposed to automatically know more than what I do. I did find out that she went by Kym. I'm not sure of her last name though. The hood called her "Bullet." "Bullet," PI repeated in a questioning manner. I just fucked a shorty over in the Wilbeth Apartments who mentioned that name. Thick politely got up off PI's lap and moved. Sorry baby he said. We all snickered. Even Thick laughed. If I'm not mistaken, he continued, she has four brothers that hangover in the Heights. They have the Reservoir area, four corners, and all of Britain sewed up. "Those lames," Lil Gucci said with no enthusiasm. "Well, sounds like we all have some work to do,' stated Reesie. Everyone agreed. We all decided that we would meet back up in 72 hours with for sure updates on everything. We need to catch these streets talking while we can. "In the meantime, Gucci started, we are about to go fill Big Ro, Bleep and Big Vee in on what's going on. We will also check in with the fam to see what's up with Dream and if they found out anything. "Okay brothers," I said as they exited my home heading for the streets.

CHAPTER SEVEN

My phone rang. It was the three guys from the club trying to hook up today. They suggested that we come by their hotel room and hang out. Reesie asked, "Hang out and do what?" That's when shit went bad. One of the guys in the background yelled" To fuck bitch, that's what! Come suck my dick and let me open that tight ass pussy you over there hiding!" Before I knew it, we were all in a shouting match, and calling each other everything under the sun. I eventually hung up and blocked them. We had shit to do.

"Well ladies," I began, let's get cleaned up so that we can hit the streets. The only way we are going to get to the bottom of what's going on in the community is to get it straight from the community. Most dudes will tell any and everything if the hopes of good pussy is involved. "Got that right," Thick agreed. "I third that," Reesie said laughing as usual, and then she said if y'all trying to fuck, why y'all just turn down the bros? We all fell out laughing and got up so that we could get moving.

Everyone went their own way. We agreed to meet back up over here in our nicest summer hoe shit. We needed answers and were willing to lie and tease our way into them. A few hours have passed. I was sitting on my couch smoking a blunt. I heard someone knocking at the door and hollered against my better judgment to "Come in." I knew damn well not to keep my door unlocked but forgot to check my locks after the girls left earlier. In walked three bitches with bats and masks. I sat still and didn't panic at all because I knew buying a few minutes of time would be lifesaving. My brothers still had my house rigged and my girls were on their way, so them talking shit and threatening didn't rattle my feathers. I continued sitting for a few more seconds until one of the hoes tried stepping into my comfort zone. My peripheral told me my backup was here, so I jumped up and started swinging. I swung, kicked, yoked hair, and swung some more. The entire time I was talking shit. The other two masked hoes tried to get a few punches in but were quickly knocked into oblivion. They never saw it coming. My brothers pulled up and broke everything up. They yoked the bitches, took off their masks, and questioned them on who sent them. At first, they wouldn't talk. A swift kick in the mouth had one saying, Bullet. We all looked at one another, not in shock, but because we all knew we had to find her.

Big Ro and Vee came inside with Lil Gucci to break up the action. Bleep was outside checking out the surroundings. Big Ro finally sat down and said, "Sis you and your girls are moving. Pack up everything y'all want in a few small boxes. We will send somebody to get your stuff by the end of the week. Until that time, you and your girls go check in at the Embassy downtown. It's paid for and y'all are all on the V.I.P. floor with security. We have a family suite on the same floor one of us will always be staying in. "I'm sick of this shit,' Big Ro continued while cracking his jaw! We have business moves to make' and now this shit is messing with my money and time. Get these bitches up and take them to where we have Meech and his dick-slinging as friends. Somebody is going to pay for all of this!

After my brothers left, we fixed ourselves back up, got our pistols, and bounced. We went from one side of town to the next looking for the money men. "BINGO," Reesie announced. It was eighty-five degrees, and everybody had their cars put up and were on their bikes. Lil Ronnies was lit. We pulled up and recognized a few friendly faces. A Dude named Cholly was on the Neiman Marcus Limited Edition. If anybody knew what was popping off, I know he knows all the underground gossip. The bitches throw panties at him just because that dude yawn. You won't get his coins though. He is tighter than Peewee Hermits drawls. Hitman had his Dodge Tomahawk out and Regg had his limited-edition Ducati Diavel out. Leonardo was leaning on his Nissan GT-R, Kevin was on his Mercedes-Benz GT-Class and Demetrius was bumping a Lexus LC while Chip pulled out his Pagani Huayna BC Roadster. They were smoking cigars and showing off their money. Lil Ronnie had his Bugatti Chiron Purr Sport under a Port so the sun wouldn't mess with his custom paint job. On the four corners of where Lil Ronnie parked were his well-trained Cane Corso's. In front was Monster and Mussolini. In the back were White Boy and Kitty.

We found a spot to park in after slow cruising thru. We wanted them to see us, just like we were peeping for them." Y'all ready ladies," I asked. "Ready as fuck" they both said in unison. We hit the blunt, threw on a little perfume, and did a walk-through. We all kind of laughed when we walked past that dude Chill and Dub leaned up on his hooptie car trying to finesse some raggedy bitches off the Northside. Thick said loud enough for anyone in earshot to hear, "with his punk ass." We screamed! Niecy is going to fuck him up." He had the nerve to holler back, "She isn't gone do shit." We all laughed and headed over to greet the others.

I felt someone breathing on me standing awfully close. My girls just stood there looking and wouldn't make a face one way or the other. I turned quickly, and it was the dude Cholly. He started laughing after saying, "What the fuck are you doing wearing booty shorts and spikes Candy?" Don't get fucked up out here trying to be fast. You got your tit's out and everything. Take your butt home before I start lighting this damn parking lot up!" We all started laughing and telling his crazy ass to go somewhere. "What's been up with y'all?" Cholly asked. We filled him in on a little bit, not much just trying to see if he had heard anything. He listened before saying, "I know enough. "What's real is what matters. Y'all are my girls, so I may have something. Hit me up later Candy." I will Cholly," I said and walked off. I saw my dude Regg watching Thick. I bumped her elbow and got her attention. Thick walked over to Regg, hesitantly because she remembered he was hugged up with Dream at the park. He started smiling knowing his ass isn't no damn good. She was smiling and talking shit through gritted teeth. This dude knows he's nothing nice, but I'm not either.

"Look at those two," I said to Reesie, and she laughed while walking in the direction of Kevin and Demetrius. I decided that I would go back and mess with Chill and Dub to see what they knew. Dub met me halfway and asked me what was up. I said" Nothing, just coming over to speak. Is that a crime?" He said, "No, but if you start any shit, it will be a crime scene." I looked him in his eyes and stepped up close enough for him to smell my breath before I answered back with, "Make your next move your best move fuck nigga! I come with the shitz. If you think for one minute you and that retarded scrub balls you swing off pump any fear in my heart, you are sadly mistaken! Now move before I bite you or push you on the ground!" Dub moved out the way quickly and yelled back to Chill that he was going inside Ronnies to see if their bitches were still coming. Chill just nodded and looked at me. "What's up Candy girl?" Chill asked. "Shit, just out here getting some air," I responded. "Air huh?" he asked sarcastically. I figured right then; he knew more. I played right along to see what was up. I could tell he either knew something or he was up to something. I was ready either way. "Yes, Air! But why did you say it like that Chill? You know how me, and you know how I get down." Chill giggled a little before responding, "Is that right? Well, since we are so tight, why haven't you given me none of that pussy? Got Meech out here tripping and trying to fuck any and everybody up about your ass girl. Shit your pussy must be lined in gold and diamonds. Especially since you haven't fucked that nigga going on two years, and he got bitches out here still looking for you and where you lay your head. Let me taste your shit Candy," He said as though he was playing, bet yet serious walking toward me smiling. Tell me more about the bitches hating on me and maybe we can schedule an edible arrangement," I responded seductively playing his game. Chill smiled and looked behind my head. The bitches he was waiting for showed up. They must be a part of Bullet's new crew. Chill laughed and said," I'm going to suck your titties watch! Call me later," He said as he walked.

I caught up with Reesie and Thick. We walked around for a little while longer until I started getting that feeling again. I looked around while putting my hand on my pistol and saw no familiar faces. This shit is driving me crazy. I want to scream so badly to whomever is following me to please show their face. Y'all ready?" I asked Thick and Reesie. They both said yes, so we walked back to the car. We all took mental pictures of who Chill was parlaying with because we knew somehow, they all were involved.

We hit Main St. and noticed that we were being followed. It was obvious as fuck! There was a girl directly behind us with one other girl in the car with her. The car behind them had three dudes in it. We saw them in the parking area we pulled out of when we left Ronni's. Every turn we made, they made. I hit Lil Gucci to see where they were. Lil Gucci said that they had just arrived at the hotel. I said head to my house ASAP we are being tailed by two cars. He asked our location, and I told him we were on the hill by the Madi block. He said they were on their way and that he would hit Big Vee, Bleep, and Big Ro up because they were up on the hill by Wildwood gambling. I said bet. Bleep ended up calling me and asking what our location was. I told him that we would be pulling up in two minutes. He said don't go to your house. Roll down to Hawkins Park, we are on the streets with our lights out. We are in a blacked-out hooptie and an all-white Kia. Pull in front of the cars and park. "Ok brother," I said," here we come. My girls were ready. All you could hear in our car was clickity clack. Thick lit a blunt and passed it around. We turned off to park in front of the park and the back glass shattered. Reesie got down and started shooting back. Thick rolled her window down and started shooting back. There was a car coming head-on in our direction that got two or three shots off before both cars blew the fuck up. My brothers lit them motherfuckas up with cannons. Thick was hit though. She sat back and hit the blunt mad as hell. Reesie took a rag we had in my car for spills and tried tying it around her arm. "I'm good," Thick said to Reesie. I think it was an in-and-out. We continued to roll away from the scene. We heard fire trucks and police in the distance. My brothers peeled out as soon as they released their cannon. We were stuck for a second and kept moving until we got to my house. We pulled into the garage and entered the house through the garage. My brothers were already there drinking and talking. Gucci informed us that Dream was doing better and that Ren and Nelli were releasing her tomorrow. They put the girls on her because they don't trust her. So, she will be under surveillance for a couple of days. Meech and his crew healed, but we still had them locked up because we hadn't decided whether we were going to kill the nucca now or use him for more info. We let the girls loose on those broads and they beat the brakes out of them. One started singing like a bird. I think Shell said the girl was one of Bullet's sisters. Bullet has a stepsister nobody knew about. She is Rican. She goes by Lyric. Lyric has been helping to run shit.

CHAPTER TEN

"This shit has gotten out of control! All behind some community dick! Lives are being lost and affected badly because he wanted to control and have what he couldn't contain. He got caught up and couldn't handle me. What is wrong with some of these niggas nowadays, I don't get it? They fuck any and everybody and then get mad when they meet a solid woman who is not willing to play the game. I supported his dreams, cooked, kept a clean and nice home, didn't run the streets, kept myself polished, and wasn't a bug-a-boo. That wasn't good enough. He went from sharing his dick with the community to trying to get physical and tear me down. The kicker was trying to destroy my property. He had to go! This is exactly why we stay single and struggle versus having struggle love."

"Sis, it's going to be ok. We men go through dumb shit to and experience the same type of pain. There are women, believe it or not, that play this same type of game. Until people accept personal accountability and stop allowing themselves to be mistreated, the only thing you can do is to continue to have standards and not settle. With that being said, we need to wrap this shit up because we have a full few days ahead of us. Y'all need to get whatever packed up, and we will figure the rest of this stuff out. So, get some rest tonight," he said. "Oh, before I forget, y'all remember that nigga Chill?" "Yeah, we know him and his sidekick Dub," they began responding. "Well, he is involved or knows who the rest of the players are. He wants an edible arrangement and claims he will sing," I began saying. "I got an edible arrangement for that scrub ass nigga. I hope he likes Pitbull's cause I got one locked up at the shop named Big Ben. Big Ben is on the verge of getting blue balls if he don't bust soon," My brother Vee blurted out. We all laughed as Bleep jumped up and said, " Man, that nigga sick, I'm out!" We all laughed as they began leaving and we said our goodbyes.

CHAPTER ELEVEN

"Alright ladies, who needs some wine and a blunt?" I asked. "Me!" Thick, and Reesie said in sequence. "We never really had the opportunity to catch up on what was said by the fellas at Lil Ronnies," I said. Thick chimed in and said, "Well, I will go first. Regg was telling me that he heard a little, but not much. He made it clear that he stays away from dumb shit. He did say though that Meech needed his ass kicked for the bullshit that he returned on. He said that he had only seen him a couple of times driving some expensive whip out in Montrose by that new cul-de-sac behind Walmart. Regg did want to know though if Meech really did that shit to Dream and I validated it. He shook his head and said Damn!"

"That must be where that Rich bitch lives and although Kevin and Demetrius didn't want to get involved either, they said to watch that nigga Chill and left it there," Reesie said. "Well, I'm about to call Cholly. He told me to call him later. I think this is late enough," I said as we all laughed. I dialed his number and put him on my intercom.

"What's going on Cholly?" "Hey Candy, how are you?" he asked. "I'm ok," I responded. "Good," he said. " Let me ask you a question," He began. "Go ahead and ask me," I responded. "Did you know that Meech and Chill are cousins?" We all looked at each other in shock as I answered back, "No, I didn't." Cholly went on to explain. "Their mothers are sisters. He said that Chill lived with Meech and his mom until he was twelve. He and Meech have been fighting over girls since they were nine years old. They both started fucking the neighborhood girls around that time. I guess Meech was getting more sex, and it started a love-hate relationship between the two. When Chill snuck and screwed Meeches sister, Coco, his first cousin, and got her pregnant that was it. He was about to turn twelve and she was eleven. Chill was sent down south to live with their grandparents until he got off the chain and they couldn't handle him anymore. He resurfaced back up here, and they both continue to battle over women. Nobody knew what ever happened to Meeches' sister or her baby."

Our mouths were still hanging. All that I could muster up to say was "Damn, Cholly do you remember the one girl he cheated on me with in the projects who got evicted?" I asked. "Yeah, I remember Bullet," he replied. "What's up with her and her people?" I asked. "Well, from what I know, when all that bullshit went down, Bullet got put out. She blamed you for that and for losing her kids. Bullet started prostituting and ended up meeting some millionaire who fell in love with her ass. He spent money changing her look, bleaching her skin, and buying her a new lifestyle. She reached out to Meech because she was still in love with him. She bought him whatever he wanted. He moved with her and started fucking all the women in her little neighborhood. From what I hear, he continued, a few of the ladies are with child. She cares less about that and cares more about if Meech is back here hooking up with you," he said. Which is the same exact story Lil Gucci had.

"I don't understand why she hates me so much," I responded trying to figure out what else he knows. "She believes you got her evicted and holds you responsible for her losing her kids, that's number one. Number two, she is obsessed with Meech. She can't get from him what she knows you own. She isn't mad at any of the other bitches because they were just fucks, it's you," he said. "Huh, I don't understand that shit because I gave him back his stuff!" I said getting irritated. "No, it's not material Candy. You own that niggas heart. He hasn't given it to anyone since you because he knew he truly fucked up. She figured that she could get rid of you by killing you. She could then have him to herself," Cholly explained.

"Can I ask you one last question Cholly, Well two?" I was pushing it. "Sure, Candy," Cholly responded. "How do you know all of this and am I in danger?" I asked because I needed to know. "Candy, all I can say is this: Keep your eyes open! Don't trust half of what you see, and it isn't over until it's over. As for how I know what I know, I will tell you another day. Today is not that day," he said. "Cholly" "Yes Candy?" "Thank you so much!" I said. "You are welcome doll! Maybe one day you'll allow a gentleman to take you out to dinner," Cholly suggested. "That's a definite date," I replied. We ended the call as I looked over at the girls whose mouths were still wide open and said, "FUCK!"

We all sat stuck. We were unsure of what to do next. Reesie suggested that we take our minds off this entire situation, work on packing our stuff, and hit the streets later. There were questions that we were determined to have answered and gaps that needed to be closed. After speaking with Cholly, we now have more questions. How in the world does he know all of this?

We all decided to help one another pack. Since we were already at my house, we started packing a few things here. I need to go back over to the U-Haul place and get a few more boxes. I was leaving a lot of stuff and buying new things. My brothers can donate my furnishings or do whatever, I don't really care. Reesie laid across my bed and lit a blunt. I knew her mind was racing when she said, "Damn, I wonder who was in those cars that were following us?" "Bitch, Thick began. "Go on your social media accounts and scroll your timeline and see who is talking or sending up R.I.P.'s social media. Shit, social media will bust a ghost out!" We all started laughing and agreeing. Reesie began scrolling her social media account and stopped to cover her mouth. "Oh my!" She turned her phone so that we could read what she had just read.

"Rest *up Coco, your murder will definitely*
Be avenged. We love you and will miss
You little sister."

"What the fuck! I hope that's a different Coco and not who I think it may be. I'm about ready to move out of this motherfuckin' town! I can't take any more of these twists and turns!" I screamed. "This shit makes know since! You thought that was bad, check this out," Reesie stated.

NEWSBREAK

The Akron Fire and Police Department were dispatched out to a known gang area last night at approximately 8:00 p.m. on the city's west side. We are still awaiting forensics as to what looks like a two-car ambush. According to an unidentified witness who happened to be walking their dog through the park, five bodies were discovered torched and unidentifiable. No names of any of the victims have been released to the public. If you have any information regarding this senseless crime, please contact CRIME STOPPERS @ 234-111-2222

We all sat frozen for a minute. Life as we knew it was about to drastically change. What upset me the most is all the people whose lives will be affected behind my choices or lack thereof. We get caught up in thinking about the "right now" not understanding that the "right now" is temporary with no time limit. Our choices in who we fuck or fuck over manipulate our choices and sometimes change our journey's destination. We all teach people how to treat us by what we allow and accept. I refused and will continue to refuse to deal with community niggas. Although I didn't catch a communicable disease, I am catching HELL! I wonder which is worse at this point.

I snapped out of my train of thought when Thick sat next to Reesie and I, and said, "Look, we are not about to give up. We are fighters and we are in this to the end. We did nothing but defend ourselves. I have a gunshot wound to prove it." Reesie jumped up and shouted, "Omg sis, I am so sorry, I should've offered to clean that up for you this morning. Let me get some peroxide, ointment, and gauze." "No! Thick replied. I'm good. I can take care of it, but thanks anyway Sis. With that being said, fuck a pity party! Let's get moving so that we can get a few things packed at my crib and Reese's. We are about to turn some corners tonight, she continued.

CHAPTER THIRTEEN

We ran by Thick and Reese's spot and got a few things packed. We showered and changed at Reese's before hitting the streets. We figured we would cruise up on the Hilltop tonight. It was a nice night to listen to some music and get our freak on. D.J. Eazy Money was on the wheels of Steel playing that old-school hip hop over at Q's joint. The owner's name was Quin, and she was not to be fucked with. Quinn was definitely sweet as hell, but no joke. I remember when I first met Quinn and began hanging out at her spot. She caught her dude cheating on her one night after closing her spot early. She recognized an unfamiliar car parked down from her house and decided to investigate for herself. Everybody on the block knew that she was one fry short of a Happy Meal, so they never fucked with her. Quinn walked around the perimeter of her house looking for evidence of an intruder or an unwelcome guest. Her gut told her something wasn't right, and according to Quinn, she follows her gut.

After looking through most of her windows, she walked up to her spare room window and almost lost it! What she saw had her wanting to commit a double homicide. She scaled the rails on the side of her porch, and in through her bathroom window. This window was often left unlocked unbeknownst to her husband, just in case of emergencies. Rumo has it that once she climbed in through the bathroom window, and made it to the bottom-level spare bedroom, she witnessed first-hand her husband having sex with a woman. Although she wanted to beat the shit out of both right then in there, she crept back out unnoticed and was able to go into the kitchen, grab a cast iron skillet, and re-enter the bedroom. She swung and knocked the bitch out cold.

She then beat her husband with it so badly, that he had multiple skull fractures, two shattered kneecaps, and no teeth. Quinn then had the audacity to yoke the girl up off of the floor, sock her in her mouth, knocking out her front teeth before asking her "if she knew whose house she was fucking in?!" When the girl answered "yes," she knocked her back out and dragged them both out to his car and put them both in the back seat. She put the car in reverse and watched it roll out into the street and hit a tree.

Needless to say, Quinn was sent to the pen for five years. Soon after, she divorced her husband on the grounds that they grew apart. She refused to take a loss and he didn't fight it; it wasn't a part of the game. She was a beast and so was the team that she built around her. Nette and Carlene are two of Quinn's sisters who have an after-hours around the back of the building. There is totally separate entrances and exits. We may have to stop in later to see what the word is, but for now, we are about to go to Quinns. D.J. Eazy Money got it jumping.

Everything was going great until those raggedy crabs from Harvard walked in. We all looked at one another because we thought a couple of them were in one of the cars that was following us the other night. I guess we were wrong. The one Niecy was fighting led the pack as they walked over by our table. She looked us up and down and said something disrespectful because all of the fish giggled. I stood up and said, "What's up Brownie?! "Do we have some unfinished business you want to handle tonight, because we can?!" She looked to her girls for confirmation or something. I have no clue, but me and my girls knew not to get it jumping in Quinns outside was free range.

"We can step outside and talk," I said before we were all in a single line headed for the exit. We hadn't stepped outside good before I blasted that bitch in her mouth. I slung her from one side of the building to the other. I heard someone screaming for us to move! I looked up, and it was my cousin crashing the scene. A few of them already had Chill hemmed up. They were beating him and Dub with a steel crowbar. The others told Thick and Reesie to get out of the way and made examples out of anybody that didn't understand.

The crowd was small outside. Most were still inside dancing. We went back in and headed to the bathroom to tighten up allowing the cousins to finish them off. After leaving the restroom, we went back out and kept walking to our car. We decided to sit in the parking lot to chill and make sure that the cousins were good, in which they were. We sat in the parking lot smoking and noticed Dream get out of the same car that she claimed she saw Meech driving the first night she saw him. On the driver's side was Lyric, Bullet's step-sister. Her car was pulled into the lot catercorner from where we sat and parked.

Cholly and Reg pulled up over there almost simultaneously and parked. They greeted one another, lit a blunt, and walked over to Lyric giving her hugs as they shared laughter. None appeared to be strangers at all.

The vibe was different. Dream walked out of Quinn and back over to where Lyric and the fellas stood laughing and talking. We also noticed that there were no signs of any altercation ever existing just moments ago. The cousins and the crowd had cleared out as though nothing ever happened. We had more questions than answers at this point. Time to bounce.

CHAPTER FOURTEEN

We ended up going over to The Drizzle, my brother's spot. We knew if we went there we could relax and be secure. It was just a regular night. So, it wasn't as jammed-packed as it would have been if they had special guests in the building. I pulled up to the valet in order to have them park my car. We entered and went straight to the V.I.P. section where we ordered our drinks, and wings with JoJo's.

The food was so damn good that we hadn't finished what we had before we began discussing ordering our to-go orders.

PI and Vee came out and sat with us. They said that we needed a meeting to catch up on what was going on. We all agreed to check into the Embassy by noon tomorrow and our meet-up would be by one.

We sat around and laughed and talked amongst one another. Feeling safe for once. We smoked on our vapes, danced, and drank until we heard the last call. Reesie leaned in and asked us if we noticed the three gentlemen sitting directly in front of us. They looked as though they'd just walked out of Vogue magazine. They had a dignified look, with a little hood, and reeking swag. Thick and I looked, and said "DAMN, who are they?" They noticed us notice them and smiled at us. We smiled and waved back. They paid their tab with one of the dancers and headed toward the exit. The lights were coming on, so we decided to do the same.

The gentlemen lingered around by the exit in order to get behind us. They took that as an opportunity to introduce themselves. "Hello," one of the gentlemen began. "My name is Twon, and these are my brothers Brian, and Les." "Glad to meet you fellas," My name is Candy," I stated. "I would like to introduce you to my friends Thick, and Reesie." "Nice to meet you, ladies," the men responded. Brian turned his attention to me and began asking "Where were you headed?" I couldn't stop cheesing, but I tried in order to respond, "Nowhere in particular." He then asked me if we'd like to go have breakfast. Before the words left his mouth Thick said, "Hell yeah!" We all laughed as they walked with us to the valet. We agreed to meet over at the all-night Waffle House on State Rd in thirty minutes and parted ways.

When we arrived, they were already seated. They all stood as we approached, greeting us with hugs and smiles. We took seats next to the gentlemen staking claim in who we wanted. I sat next to Brian, Reesie sat next to Twon, and Thick and Les took seats next to one another. We laughed and talked in between ordering and eating. Time was flying past fast. They asked questions about our personal lives. As we asked the same. We found out that they were in town on business for two weeks. They all grew up in the same neighborhood and attended the same college. All attended college on Athletic Scholarships. One became a chemist, another an attorney, and the last was an owner of several funeral home franchises. "Very impressive," Reesie said aloud to no one in particular.

This made the guys chuckle a little before we were rudely distracted by some loud ghetto voices. In walks Cholly, and Regg with Lyric, and Dream. Reesie was the first to say, "Uggh." Everyone chuckled again except for Thick. She kept looking over at Regg and Cholly calling them corny. Corny and lame with trifling hoes. Something was a little off. We noticed that the guys we were with began acting jittering and uneasy. I glanced over a few times and noticed Cholly was watching our table. What's also strange to me is the fact that he never acknowledged us at all. I began to wonder if the things he told me over the phone were true or if it was something he fabricated to take me off a trail. Watching and seeing him lately makes me wonder what is really going on. I must make a mental note to ask my brothers what's up with Meech and do they still have those chics that came to my house.

"Well ladies," Brian began announcing. "We are about to head out. We have an early morning we need to prepare for. "We're heading out as well," Thick stated. We all got up and exited the restaurant promising to keep in touch and possibly hook up in the next couple of days. We pulled out of the parking lot and headed home. That is when I discovered my phone was missing. I pulled back up into the driveway and ran back inside to see if I had left it where we sat. I could have accidentally dropped it. Either way, I was praying someone would turn it in. I remembered having it at the table, but I couldn't find it anywhere. I looked under the table and in the area of our table. I eventually asked the busser and server if they saw a phone. They said, "No." I left back out pissed and confused. We were all exhausted and ready to go lay down after searching the car and my purse once more. We've had a long day and couldn't wait to pull out and head back to the hotel. "I'll have the damn phone turned off and shut down!" I began saying. "I'll just get up in the morning, and head out to get a new one."

As we approached the exit, We noticed some real fuck shit! Cholly had Lyric bent over fuckin her from the back, while Lyric ate out Dream. Dream looked like a person with intellectual disabilities standing with her legs cocked open getting ate out, while jacking off Regg. Now this is some hoe shit for real! This is super low even for these hoes! There is no way in hell that any of this should be going down out in public for all to see. This has truly made me look at Regg and Cholly in a new light! Too bad I don't believe in calling the police because I swear that I would turn all of their asses in for indecent exposure, prostitution, and any other charge I could think of! I got out of the car and stood long enough for them to see or feel me in their presence, not that it would make a difference to any of them. I shook my head and returned to the car as soon as they saw me. I peeled out of the parking lot and headed to the hotel cursing both Regg and Cholly out in my head. They are just as disgusting as the bitches they were fucking as far as I was concerned, Cholly can lose my number!

We arrived at the hotel and my brothers were there still up waiting for our return. They heard us as we exited the elevator talking. They made their way over to our room. "What's up, brothers?" All of them answered, "Nothing in sequence." Lil Gucci is the nosey brother. So, I knew it was coming. "Where y'all been?" he asked right on time. We filled them in on everything from leaving the club, the guys, and breakfast as well as what we witnessed with Cholly, Regg, Dream, and Lyric. Lil Gucci shook his head and then asked about the fight earlier. We went on to explain what went down before Big Ro and Vee interrupted and said, "Y'all need to sit yawls hot asses down somewhere!" Thick turned to Big Ro and Vee and said, "Shut the fuck up!" Before they could say anything back, PI walked over to Thick and said, "Don't do that!" She looked at him as though she didn't know what he was talking about. She then said, "Do what?" PI leaned down in her face and said sternly, "That shit!" She was mad, but she didn't say anything else.

Thick lit a blunt and sat back while mumbling, "Big ass bully!" I thought the shit was funny. Those two crack me up. This opened the floor for me to ask them what was going on with Meech and his boys, the girls, and the cannon incident. Big Vee took over and said, "We are releasing Meech and his boys as we speak. They shouldn't be causing any more problems. The girl's Bullet sent was released yesterday. They won't be visiting anyone else. The cousins, Aunt Ren, and Nelly are taking responsibility for them hoes. One of the girls we found out who perished in the car was Meeches' little sister Coco. Bullet must have put her own her team."

"None of that is pointing in our direction. Not even the witness who was walking in the park could identify us. Our cars went to the scrap and are officially scrapped out. Oh, the car you drove that night was scrapped out too. Sorry, Sis, we will buy you another one. Our businesses have been raided twice for tax evasion, and we are under investigation for running an alleged prostitution ring out of Drizzle. We need y'all to stay under the Radar Sis," Vee began saying. "Everywhere y'all tend to go y'all stirring up some more damn problems. It is hard for us to resolve one situation before we are trying to put the fire out of something else. As for Cholly and Regg, we aren't worried about them. They are doing what they do. Dream and Lyric, we have someone on them. Chill for a while, and go to a movie or go shopping, DAMN, just stop getting in shit!" he yelled. "Well damn, I guess If I told y'all my phone is missing I'd be pushing it, I said. Big Ro spoke up and asked, "Where is the last place you had it?" "At breakfast. We went to breakfast with the guys we met at the

Drizzle." Big Ro just stared at me cracking his jaw for what seemed like several minutes but, it was seconds. He told Lil Gucci to call security at the club and tell them to roll the tape back. He asked me the approximate time which was easy because it was almost closing. They were able to get a clip sent to Lil Gucci's phone in a matter of seconds. They all looked at one another in shock, jumped up, and left not saying a word.

We decided that we would go chill by the pool for the rest of the day. We chilled drinking our wine and smoking. PI and Lil Gucci showed up and brought me a new phone. They also informed us that we needed to get dressed in some sexy scandal because we ladies were going on a date. We looked at one another in shock. Thick asked, "Who's going on a date? I'm not doing shit!" PI was becoming irritated with Thick lately. She was talking out and he is the one brother who will not tolerate a woman talking shit like that. "Woman Shut the fuck up and you are!" he yelled. We all burst out laughing at how those two were acting toward one another, yet again.

"This is the deal, those three guys you all entertained that night are hired assassins in town to kill for Bullet. We heard she had people coming but we were unsure of who or when. It's a good thing they stole your other phone Candy. Yeah, they stole it, because we had a tracker on it and were able to track them and Bullet out in Montrose. We must kill that bitch before she kills everyone to get to you, Candy. All these issues over that community dick as nigga! Our inside sources also told us that Meech went against our little agreement because he thinks he's invincible. He also blames Candy for his sister's death. He swears she killed her to get back at him for not wanting her, and for smashing Dream.

CHAPTER SEVENTEEN

Phones started ringing and everyone was looking around to see whose it was. "Hello," Big Vee answered. He sat there with a disturbed but confused look on his face. He asked, "Did anyone see anything or know who ordered the hit? That's what's up!" he said before hanging up his line. We went from listening to Big Vee to listening to Lil Gucci on the phone. We caught the end of his conversation as he said, "I knew sooner or later that dude's fate was going to be his death. Alright BET!" We looked on waiting on one or both to catch up to speed. Reesie stood up pacing back and forth mumbling something under her breath.

Lil Gucci watched unsure of whether to get up and try talking to her or whether to let her just pace and think. In the meantime, Big Vee started out by saying, "Chill and Dub were killed on Harvard last night. They said some dudes killed them execution style. Bullet was shot at and hit in the leg and butt and her assassins were found tied up in the back of the Save More on Copley. They were shot multiple times and set on fire." Thick screamed, "Oh hell nawl!" Does anybody know anything else?" Big Vee asked. "Not one damn thing," Lil Gucci began responding. "But that's not all. Although Bullet was only injured earlier; her millionaire man was found dead in their garage. I guess a neighbor saw smoke coming from under the garage door and lifted it. The car was running and accelerated on high with a brick on the gas. The fumes killed him. The police took her shot-up body in for questioning and began questioning her about her wounds. She was released to her attorney and told not to go anywhere. They would be keeping in touch.

Meech is planning revenge for his sister's death according to our inside source. "Who the fuck is this inside source?" I asked. "You will know in due time," Big Ro responded cracking his damn jaw. "That is so irritating," I mumbled." Y'all get your stuff and let's head back to the rooms," PI ordered. Thick parted her mouth to say something and PI walked over to her and said, "Say something so that I can prove who the man is around this motherfucka'!" She just looked at him and walked off. Reesie and I got in line right behind her saying not one damn thing. "Get online and let's see what the word is Reesie," I said. Let me plug my phone in, "she responded. The first thing Reesie noticed was the post regarding Meech's sister's memorial service.

A memorial service will be held on Tuesday, June 11, 2021, at Stumble Block
funeral home for Coco Jenkins from 2:00 p.m. to 4:00 p.m.
Please forward any cards or flowers to the funeral home
located at:
77793 N. Exchange St.
Akron Ohio 33375

CHAPTER EIGHTEEN

"Damn, that was fast!" I said. My brothers entered with food, wine, and weed. We had strict orders to stay put. We were also told that we were going to be babysat just in case we had some sneaky ideas of sneaking out. We all laughed and said, "BABYSITTER?" PI said, "That's what we said!" He then got on his phone and said, "Come on up and then hung up." A few minutes later we heard a knock at the door. Big Ro got up and opened the door. If looks could kill those two would be dead. In walks Cholly and Regg. I jumped up and said, "What the fuck is really going on?!" Cholly looked at me with disdain before saying, "Shut the fuck up Candy and sit your ass down. We have all night to talk." I had an instant attitude. Thick again parted her mouth to say something more and PI cut his eyes her way. She just sat back and ate her ribs. I didn't give a fuck! I spoke up for myself! "First of all, you block-headed motherfucka', to whom the fuck you talking too! That was rude and uncalled for! Secondly, if you must keep us company, we need to set some rules up front! There won't be any disrespecting any of us anymore by you or anyone else! I looked over at my brother PI as well.

We demand respect, we aren't asking or begging! Don't ask for more than you're willing to give, and if you come with the shits, you will be shitted on! PERIOD! With that being said, we can start this over fresh or pick up where I'm about to leave off. It's your choice." I'm sorry Ladies, will you accept my apology?" Cholly responded. PI stood up and said, "Fuck y'all, and your gonna do what the fuck I say without an apology, or you will wish you had." We just rolled our eyes at him. He definitely has mental issues.

Regg chimed in and extended his apology as well. My brothers laughed and said that they would check in with us later, the streets were about to be a war zone. We all hugged and said, "I love you" and our goodbyes for now.

Cholly and Regg sat down after fixing themselves a drink and Regg rolling a blunt. Cholly began talking first. He turned and looked at me. "Remember when we spoke, and you asked me how I knew what was going on Candy?" "Yes, I remember," I said. "Meech is my stepbrother. His mother married a few times and my father happened to be one of those men. He and I never got along, but to keep the peace I avoided him as much as possible. Regg and I both met while working undercover. We've been on Meech and Bullet, well "Kym" for years. Right when we get close enough to get them, they wiggle out. We got Dream to turn informant. She has been wired ever since the rape. We were kind of forced into what you saw at the restaurant because Lyric was on to us. She was working with the assassins you all were eating breakfast with. In order to prevent them from killing y'all that night, we had to go in deep." "Regg and Cholly dapped and laughed. We looked at them without cracking one damn smile. "We have Lyrics line tapped, so when they called and said they had your phone Regg was listening through his earpiece. Regg then chimed in, "Dream was pissed and is still pissed. She did not want to do any of that sex shit. She only did it and allowed the wire because she feels like she owes y'all for saving her life."

"We took Kym in for questioning in the death of her millionaire pimp." Thick interrupted and asked, "Well, who killed Chill and Dub does anyone have any leads?" "No leads," Regg replied. That's a mystery because they fucked over so many people. "Who killed the assassins?" Reesie asked, "We are clueless," Cholly began. "It is imperative that we keep eyes on Lyric and keep her close by. She's Bullets eyes and ears on the streets," he continued." I thought about all of what was just told, and then it dawned on me, "Well then who's watching Bullet tonight while you two Robo cops are here with us?" Cholly looked at Regg and then back at us without saying a word. "Big Ren, Nelly, Shell, Ya, and Tip," Regg responded. "Oh shit," We all finally laughed because we knew that one false move with any of the fam would land both Bullet and Lyric in a lake. "Candy, I want to say this and get it off my chest," Cholly began. He grabbed my hand and said with a straight face, "Look Candy, you deserve a man that is going to treat you like a Queen and appreciate you and what you bring to the table. You deserve a man who will protect you and provide for you. You do not deserve a community dick ass nucca that's going to bring drama and harm your way." I interrupted his speech because it was making me feel all mushy inside." Thank you Cholly," I said. "When this is all over with, I would like to ask you out on a real date," he continued. "Well, Cholly," I'm not sure about that. I don't think I could get use to my man going undercover and screwing suspects," I said with a straight face. Regg cleared his throat and looked over at Thick who was scrolling on her phone looking on Fb. "I swear that was the first and only time I have ever done that," he responded. "Wrong promise!" I came back with. "You should be over here promising never to do it again," I said with a smile on my face.

Reesie laughed just as Thick screamed for me to call and check in with my brothers. "Something just went down! Somebody went live at Club Drizzle and there are fire trucks and police everywhere!" Thick shouted. I panicked and couldn't think. I tried calling several times repeatedly receiving no answer. Cholly ended up making the call and found out that Bullet and Meech were suspected of planting a stick of dynamite in the parking garage attached to the Drizzle and blowing it up.

Lil Gucci and Big Ro were out on the streets handling business at the time. The car Meech had been driving exited the parking garage first, seconds later they heard a BOOM and witnessed the entire thing blow up. Big Vee and PI are in surgery, Bleep is in ICU fighting for his life. "OMG, I screamed!!! No, not my brothers! I'm killing those two myself I screamed in between tears. I need to call the family I said in between sniffles." I called Big Ren and explained all I knew, she was livid. She told me she would call me back after she spoke to everyone. I hung up with her, curled up in my chair, and prayed for my brothers. Within the hour everyone in town was on Facebook talking and repeating different versions of what they'd heard. Big Ren and Nelly had the family all meet up at the hospital. They made us stay put and called in their own reinforcement to guard the parking garage at the hospital while they all took position inside. They left the stake out at Lyrics just as Meech and Bullet showed up to hide out. They were laughing and bragging before they were grabbed up and blinded with pillowcases. Lyrics front and back door was kicked in almost simultaneously. Tear gas was set off to smoke her out and she was smoked out. She was shot execution style as was Bullet and Meech. The invaders escaped as fast as they came shooting cannons at the property and blowing it to smithereens.

Big Ren called after a couple of hours to let us know that PI and Big Vee made it out of surgery. Bleep is still in ICU and Lil Gucci and Big Ro are spastic and up there with them. The police keep trying to question everyone and we don't know anything more than what was seen. "Hello, Hello Big Ren are you there?" "Yes, I'm here," Big Ren began responding. "What's up?" she said. "I thought I saw somebody I knew. Lord, my eyes are playing tricks on me. I will call you once I have more updates," the caller said before hanging up.

Big Vee was in a private room. The door cracked open, and he popped his head in. "I needed to see that you are alive and that all your vitals had improved," he atated before kissing Big Vee's forehead, and saying, "I'll be back as he exited." He headed next door to PI's room and entered. "Your vitals are steady, which is a good sign. Both of you are strong and healthy, and will pull through," he said as he kissed PI's forehead. "I will be back," he continued saying as he exited the room heading down to Bleeps in ICU. "He's doing much better, and his vitals are up," he began saying once again before he kissed Bleep's forehead. "I will be back," he whispered and turned to exit, but not before Bleep opened his eyes and said," DAD!" "Yes, son." "When did you get out?" Bleep asked. "Well son, I've been home long enough to do some damage that could send me back for life. I am leaving town after I make sure you all are ok. Please don't mention you've seen me. You boys won't have any more problems. I made sure of it," their dad said. "That's what's up Dad!" "Is Candy still hiding at that hotel with her sexy friends?" he asked. "Dad, how did you know where any of us were?" Bleep questioned. "I have been following you guys and lightweight stalking you. I think I started spooking Candy out. My baby could feel my presence but didn't recognize me. Her paranoia made me get busy, so I got those disrespectful punks on Harvard first. Talking to my daughter like she ain't shit! That pissed me off. I got that bitch Meech, his bitch Bullet, her rich man, and that girl that was with them. I blew them bitches up!" Dad said.

"My biggest dilemma right now is figuring out how to see my other boys out there in the waiting area. I got to get past your crazy aunts and cousins. They are certified crazy!" Dad said. We both laughed. "Well Dad, I love you! If you go slide down a side hall, I can get a nurse to bring them in and you can get at Lil Gucci and Big Ro," Bleep suggested. "Alright son. See you sooner than later." "Alright pops."

"Hey, Bleep, how are you feeling?" Aunty Nelli asked. "I am sore Aunty Nelli, but I'm going to make it," I responded. "Good Big Ren and Nelli both said." "I think I need some rest and a blunt because I swear my mind is playing tricks on me up in here today! I can't get the image out of my head 'cause I swear I saw yawls daddy crazy aged ass!" Ren said. "Aunty you are dreaming," I began replying. "Stop smoking that dirt weed." We all started laughing. My cousins took the remote and turned the TV on just in time for the news. It showed Bullet's house being blown up and the news reporter saying that they were shot execution-style before being torched in the house. It was verified that the deceased were two women and one man. The reporter asked, "If anyone saw anything or knows anything to contact the Akron Police Dept." Everyone's mouth dropped. We couldn't believe what we had just heard.

Right then in there, I was happy as hell! Although Pops wasn't always here, he showed up when we needed him the most. This made me more determined to heal and get the fuck out of this hospital in order to spend more time with him. Maybe this is our opportunity to get our lives together before it is too late.

I would love to just settle down, and chill with my girl and live to enjoy a few children. Maybe I will buy a house further out and just enjoy my family and dad. Getting the fuck away from the same community, and doing the same shit, can be a costly lesson.

"I'm killing all of them motherfuckas," Lil Gucci said. Big Ro just sat cracking his jaw. He noticed a man staring at him, and he whispered to Lil Gucci, "Look up nigga." He did and Lil Gucci almost went in shock. They both got up and exited the hospital behind the man. "Hey, wait up old school!" The man turned around and said," I'm still your daddy boy," as he smiled at both boys. They were so happy that they tried picking him up and hugging him all at the same time. "What's up, man? When did you touch down?!" they both questioned their dad. "Well, like I just told Bleep," their dad began. "I've been here long enough to cause myself enough trouble to send me back to jail for life." "What could you have done already Dad?" Ro asked. "The Lord knows," he began. "Let's just say that my kids shouldn't be having any more problems. Go talk to Bleep, I filled him in on everything already. Boys, I need to get out of here and go see Candy before I go into hiding for a while. I will be back and forth," Dad said. "Let me call and get her to meet you somewhere. I won't tell her you are at home, Dad. We have two cops up there babysitting her, so it would be too risky for you to go up to the room," Lil Gucci stated.

"Boy, If you don't call those two sorry-ass cops and tell them to come down here to this hospital, you'll wish you had! I'm going to go see my baby dammit! I have been watching her from a distance for a while. It's time that I hug my baby and tell her that I love and miss her. Now get on the damn phone and make it happen!" their dad said in a direct order. "She looks just like your momma," their dad began. I didn't respect and protect ya mama like I should have, otherwise, she would still be here. The streets was my bitch, and I showed the streets more love, and I'm sorry for my choices! If anything, ever happens to me, I need for you boys to take better care of my baby girl and love her above these streets! Do ya understand?" Lil Gucci looked on at him with sadness. Thinking about how much time they've missed out on not having a dad present in their lives. Things have got to change! Taking better care of one another and enjoying life has to trump this street shit going forward. I want to settle down one day and not have to continue looking over my shoulders. At this motherfucking point, hell I just want to grow old. Interrupting Lil Gucci's thoughts their dad said, "Nigga did you hear what I said?" "Sorry about that old school! We are calling, and we heard every word you said, damn!" Big Ro replied chuckling a little bit at Lil Gucci being stuck, and because he knew that their dad would still challenge them at his older age if they didn't do what he said. "Good," dad began saying sternly. "That's a better plan anyway!" "Here Dad," Big Ro gave him a stack of money. "Go find you a house and put this down. Let us know when you have found one that you like. We can have some furnishings delivered and take you to get some new clothes and a ride of your choosing," Alright son, I will. He stood taking in his boys and how much they had matured before saying, "Take care until I see y'all again. I love you boys!"

"Hey Cholly, what's going on?" Lil Gucci asked. "Nothing, Lil Gucci. We are just chilling. Why, what's up?" Cholly asked. "What are the girls up to?" Lil Gucci questioned. "They are all passed out," Cholly responded. "Cool, why don't you and Regg come down here to the hospital so that we can catch up? The girls should be ok," Lil Gucci suggested. "We will be there in ten minutes." Cholly and Regg left just in time. As they exited the elevator heading for the parking lot, Dad jumped on heading up to see his baby. He searched his pockets looking for his medication, forgetting he had left it in the car. It appears lately; that he was overexerting himself.

He never wanted his kids to know how sickly he really was. He also couldn't leave this earth without avenging some of his deepest secrets. His mission was accomplished, and he felt as though he had vindicated himself a little. He had one more obstacle to cross and that was with his baby girl. Although he loved all of his children, Candy was her mother reincarnated in his eyes. He knew that the boys were protecting her, but it was up to him to save her.

Feeling partially to blame for everything Candy and the boys have gone through, he knew now was the time to show up and handle his business like a father should. He wanted to protect his seeds at any cost. His body was growing tired, and he knew that he needed some rest, or he would be back in the hospital. He approached the door and knocked waiting for Candy to open up. He knocked again, and finally, the door flung open. Candy looked sleepily at him as he looked at her. His eyes began to water when she said, "Daddy!?" He said, "Yes, baby." She grabbed him and held him as she cried. He held on doing the same.

Candy walked their dad into the hotel room closing the door behind them. She asked Reesie and Thick could they give them some privacy and they both agreed they'd go down to the bar or pool area for a while. This gave Candy and her dad all the privacy they needed.

Their dad caught her up on the details of his arrival. He began with his arrival, and where he'd been staying. "Candy, I would periodically watch you and the boys when I first arrived. I wanted to get your routines down-packed. It bothered me to watch you become paranoid by my actions. I had to get involved somehow, so I chose to do what I know best and that was to kill. It was my responsibility as your father to handle everything and everyone involved trying to hurt my babies. Once I accomplished that baby girl, I could go sit down and heal," he explained. Candy looked lovingly at her father with continued tears of joy streaming down her face. She desperately needed her daddy. "I love you so much Dad! Please don't leave anymore. I missed you so much, now that you are home, I couldn't imagine not having you back in our lives. " He wiped her face before saying, "Baby girl, I have to go away until everything blows over and my health improves. I wasn't going to come home before I healed. Your daddy has a bad heart and couldn't pass up the opportunity when that detective guy reached out to me and kept me posted on what was going on back here. I had to do something. So, when I got released, Instead of going to get treatment, I came here first and laid low. I watched from afar and felt how uneasy it was making you, and how much bullshit it was causing my boys, "Dad continued explaining.

"I was pissed at Kym, Bullet, whatever y'all called the hoe! I was going to kill the hoe despite all the other shit that transpired. Kym was one of my bottom bitches back in the day." Candy looked at her dad in shock after he said what he said but knew not to interrupt. "She was as young as you," he continued. "It made me shame, but not enough to take her off of the block. She claims her kids were my seeds." "WHAT!?" Candy yelled! Being in shock was an understatement. She knew that she had to listen, and not continue to interrupt. "You heard me right baby, but we never got blood work, and I couldn't let your momma find out. I denied them and sent her straight to the projects. I stopped taking care of her, so she tried getting back at me by messing with you and your nigga."

"Kym knew eventually I would come out and avenge this bullshit! I plan to travel back and forth once I settle down somewhere," he explained. I sat quietly in thought. I was unsure of how to digest all of this, but I needed answers from my dad. Now that he explained, I figured it would be the perfect time to get a few answers. "Dad, this was a lot to digest at one time. You just basically said that Kym's kids could possibly be our siblings. Do you plan to have them tested? That's the first question, and the second question, you stated that a detective kept you posted on us. What detective have you been in contact with?" I asked. "He's the one I got rolling with your brothers. Detective Cholly," my dad responded. "What! I am so fucking confused at this point. None of this makes sense!" I yelled. "It won't baby," my dad responded. "I was once considered community dick, and a womanizer. Your beautiful mother did not deserve any of what I did or was doing. I loved her dearly, but I loved these streets equally. I met that detective when he contacted me about another situation I was fighting. We would have long talks. One evening we were shooting the shit, and he began telling me about a girl that he'd fallen madly in love with. Her name was Candy. I would listen as he spoke of you. I allowed him to feel comfortable enough to open up to me. He then began talking about the boys and the rest is history. "Wow!" is all I could think to say. I laid my head on my daddy's shoulder as he wrapped his arms around me. Still uncertain of the future because he avoided answering the question regarding the D.N.A. of Kym's children. We both just sat in silence until we drifted off to sleep. Reesie and Thick returned and woke me up. I tried waking up daddy and he wouldn't wake up. "Daddy, wake up! Wake up Daddy," I cried out as I laid on his chest and took in his scent. Thick called the paramedics as my brothers arrived and we laid back against the couch replaying our last conversations with him. Is this over, or will Kym's kids blame us and eventually want to avenge their mother's death?